Dear Parent:
Your child's love of reading starts here!

Every child learns to read in a different way and at his or her own speed. Some go back and forth between reading levels and read favorite books again and again. Others read through each level in order. You can help your young reader improve and become more confident by encouraging his or her own interests and abilities. From books your child reads with you to the first books he or she reads alone, there are I Can Read Books for every stage of reading:

SHARED READING
Basic language, word repetition, and whimsical illustrations, ideal for sharing with your emergent reader

BEGINNING READING
Short sentences, familiar words, and simple concepts for children eager to read on their own

READING WITH HELP
Engaging stories, longer sentences, and language play for developing readers

READING ALONE
Complex plots, challenging vocabulary, and high-interest topics for the independent reader

ADVANCED READING
Short paragraphs, chapters, and exciting themes for the perfect bridge to chapter books

I Can Read Books have introduced children to the joy of reading since 1957. Featuring award-winning authors and illustrators and a fabulous cast of beloved characters, I Can Read Books set the standard for beginning readers.

A lifetime of discovery begins with the magical words "I Can Read!"

Visit www.icanread.com for information
on enriching your child's reading experience.

Charlotte's Web™

WILBUR FINDS A FRIEND

Adapted by Jennifer Frantz

Illustrated by Aleksey and Olga Ivanov

Based on the Motion Picture

Screenplay by Susanna Grant and Karey Kirkpatrick

Based on the book by E. B. White

HarperCollins*Publishers*

HarperCollins®, 🐷®, and I Can Read Book® are trademarks of HarperCollins Publishers.

Charlotte's Web: Wilbur Finds a Friend

™ & © 2006 Paramount Pictures Corp. All rights reserved. Printed in the United States of America. No part of this book may be used or reproduced in any manner whatsoever without written permission except in the case of brief quotations embodied in critical articles and reviews. For information address HarperCollins Children's Books, a division of HarperCollins Publishers, 1350 Avenue of the Americas, New York, NY 10019. www.icanread.com

Library of Congress catalog card number: 2006920330
ISBN-10: 0-06-088282-4 (trade bdg.) — ISBN-13: 978-0-06-088282-2 (trade bdg.)
ISBN-10: 0-06-088281-6 (pbk.) — ISBN-13: 978-0-06-088281-5 (pbk.)

❖

First Edition

Some people say a barn is
empty without a pig in it.
But the Arables' barn
was quite full.

They had just gotten a very special pig.

His name was Wilbur.

Wilbur was a sweet little pig.

He was born on a clear spring day.

He was the runt of the litter.

That means that Wilbur was smaller

than his brothers and his sisters.

Fern Arable had saved Wilbur.

Fern's father had said he was

too small to survive.

But Fern knew better.

Fern's father did not want
to take care of a runt.
He would not let her keep Wilbur.
Wilbur had to go live on her uncle's farm.
But Fern could still visit.

Wilbur was lonely in this new place,
without his friend.

Wilbur decided it was time
to make a new friend in the barn.
But who?

There was Ike the horse, who thought

he was the boss of the barn.

And Gussy and Golly,

two geese who were always

fussing at each other.

There were Betsy and Bitsy,

two cows who loved to gossip.

And Samuel the sheep,

who was always followed by all

the other sheep on the farm.

And then, there was Templeton the rat.

But all he cared about was food.

In a barn full of animals,
Wilbur still felt alone . . .

until something special happened.

It was nighttime,

and Wilbur was too lonely to sleep.

"Good night," he called

to the other animals.

But there was just silence.

"Good night?" Wilbur said again sadly.

Then a voice answered

from the darkness.

Wilbur pricked up his ears.

"Who said that?" he asked.

"Me," said the voice.

Wilbur wanted to keep talking.

But the voice said it was time to sleep.

They could talk more the next day.

Wilbur was so excited

it took him a while to fall asleep.

The next morning, Wilbur
was eager to find his new friend.
Wilbur called out.
"I will come down," the voice said.

Then suddenly Wilbur saw her—
a great big spider!
The other animals in the barn
moved away at the sight of her.
They had always thought
she was just an ugly spider
and they never wanted to be her friend.

"Salutations," the spider said to Wilbur.

"I am Charlotte."

"*Salu . . . ?*" Wilbur mumbled.

He did not understand such a big word.

"It means hello,"
Charlotte said kindly.
"Oh! Hello!" Wilbur said
with a big smile.

And with those few words,
a friendship began.

Where the other animals saw just a spider,

Wilbur saw kindness and beauty.

He was happy to have a new friend.

They were an unlikely pair.
Who would have thought
that a pig and a spider
would become friends?

But Wilbur and Charlotte
would become the *best* of friends.
Charlotte worked hard spinning her
webs to show everyone how special
Wilbur was.

Wilbur saw that Charlotte
was gentle and caring.
And slowly, so did all of the
other animals.

And Charlotte knew
that Wilbur's kind heart
truly made him . . .